D0463492

SAM SILVERSTEIN

THE LOST COMMANDMENTS

OTHER BOOKS BY SAM SILVERSTEIN

The Success Model

No More Excuses

Nonnegotiable

Making Accountable Decisions

No Matter What

SAM SILVERSTEIN

THE LOST COMMANDMENTS

SOUND WISDOM
P.O. Box 310
Shippensburg, PA 17257-0310

For more information on publishing and distribution rights, call 717-530-2122 or info@soundwisdom.com.

Quantity Sales. Special discounts are available on quantity purchases by corporations, associations, and others. For details, contact the Sales Department at Sound Wisdom.

While efforts have been made to verify information contained in this publication, neither the author nor the publisher assumes any responsibility for errors, inaccuracies, or omissions.

While this publication is chock-full of useful, practical information, it is not intended to be legal or accounting advice. All readers are advised to seek competent lawyers and accountants to follow laws and regulations that may apply to specific situations.

The reader of this publication assumes responsibility for the use of the information. The author and publisher assume no responsibility or liability whatsoever on behalf of the reader of this publication.

ISBN 13 HC: 978-1-64095-012-2
ISBN 13 Ebook: 978-1-64095-013-9

For Worldwide Distribution, Printed in the U.S.A.
1 2 3 4 5 6 7 8 / 21 20 19 18

Cover/Jacket designer Geoff Silverstein
Interior design by Terry Clifton

DEDICATION

To Renee

CHAPTER 1

I drifted somewhere between the sound sleep I desired and the wakefulness I dreaded.

Please let me sleep just a little bit longer, I thought to myself.

My senses started to awaken as well, and I began to feel that same warm touch that I felt so many mornings in the past. Why Renee and I bought a home with skylights in the bedroom I'll never know. Tuesday was the one day I could sleep in. I didn't have to teach until one o'clock, and I was in no hurry to get going. The only problem was that by 8:30, the sun had climbed high enough into the sky to shine down through those irritating skylights and concentrate right on my eyelids. The warmth spread across my face and actually started to feel good as I completely came out of my deep slumber and fully realized where I was.

As I lay in bed staring up at the white ceiling and bright skylights above me, I listened to the peaceful humming of the heater and the faint chirping of the birds outside the windows. There were no showers running, no drawers slamming, and no children shouting. There were no feet running down the hallway, no hairdryers blowing, and no cereal being fought over.

Tuesday morning was my time. Renee was on her way to work, the children were at school, and it was quiet at home. I rolled out of bed, brushed my teeth, and decided to go for a run. I slipped on my shorts, T-shirt, and socks, grabbed my running shoes, and went out the back door.

Turning left out of the driveway, I headed up the street for my regular six-mile run. Even after a dozen marathons I still enjoyed getting out for a relaxing jaunt. It was a perfect 50 degrees this March morning, a real runner's delight. As my feet pounded methodically against the pavement, my mind drifted from issue to issue; and before I knew it, I was almost back at home. My mind wandered from thoughts about the kids' soccer teams, to global issues at hand, to everything in between. Everything that is, except the road in front of me. But my feet seemed to know the way, and through all my years of running I've always managed to evade harm's way.

After a quick shower, I slipped into some khakis and a navy-blue shirt, and I headed into the kitchen for breakfast. I poured my usual bowl of Honey Nut Cheerios, skim milk, and a tall glass of orange juice. I felt fortunate to have orange juice this morning as Geoff, my oldest child and only son, usually beats me to it and finishes off the jug before I'm even awake. As I set my food on the kitchen table and sat down in my regular chair, I noticed an envelope sitting right in the middle of the table. I hadn't seen it before I went running.

Maybe Renee left me a note, I thought.

Occasionally she'll jot me a note with a phone message or a reminder for the afternoon; however, as I picked up the envelope, I began to doubt that it came from her. The envelope looked old and yellowed. It felt brittle in my fingers. I opened it and read the following message:

The second ten exist. Trust your instincts.
Find Ayn in the old city. It
is time. You will see.

It looked like one of the thousands of art projects that my two youngest daughters, Allison and Jackie, worked on together. At seven and nine it seemed that a crayon or marker was always in their hands.

Maybe it was hidden under the newspaper earlier, I thought, *that's why I didn't notice it before I went out to run.*

But this paper looked and felt so old.

How did they get the paper to look like this, I wondered.

I ate breakfast, read the newspaper, and cleared the table. I threw everything away, including the kids' art project. Although we usually keep a sampling of their work, if Renee and I saved every project that the kids did, we would need a separate home just to house it all. The fridge was already overflowing with drawings, paintings, and the obligatory hand outlines they made at school.

I wanted to get to my office before my one o'clock class started. It was only History 101 but I always liked to pick out a new reading and share it with the class. There was such an abundance of resources at the office that I rarely needed to look for articles at home.

I don't know why I bother to take my briefcase home, I thought.

I did much of my research on campus, and my lesson plan was always completed in advance and placed inside the briefcase. I could just as easy leave it in my office and pick it up on the way to class, but somehow the case always found its way into my car. I picked up the worn black attaché case sitting next to the back door and headed to the Washington University campus.

The drive down Highway 40 was spectacular. Embankments on both sides of the highway were overflowing with yellow jonquils. It was a sea of yellow guiding the road toward campus. I drove up Forsyth and turned left into the parking lot. As I parked my car on campus, I noticed that flowers were starting to pop up all over. Beds of tulips, lined in neat rows, added color everywhere. Spring really was my favorite time of year. The harsh winter had passed and it was easier to get out and run. Spring break was next week, exams would follow shortly, and summer vacation was in sight. I walked briskly down the stone path into Rosemont Hall, up to the second floor and into room 203, my office.

I flipped through my mail. It was filled with the usual amount of junk that I tossed aside, leaving the rest in a neat pile on my desk to be opened and read after class. I reached down, grabbed my briefcase with the enclosed lesson plan, and headed to class.

History 101 was always a big class. There were more than 250 students in the lecture hall. Many of them were history majors, but a fair amount of the students were not. The class was made up of mostly freshmen and sophomores with a few juniors sprinkled in. This particular classroom was curved in shape, and the seats rose from the floor where I stood. As I looked up and around the room, I saw the familiar faces of my students. These young adults came to college with high aspirations. They came not only to get an education and start their career, but they also came to learn more about themselves and their place in this world. Equally important to many, they came to meet new people, explore new experiences, and have an incredible time in the process. My privilege was interacting with them in an environment that allowed them to deliberate on issues outside of those traditionally addressed in a history class; it was to challenge them to approach ideas in a new way. My goal was for them to leave class with the ability to delve deeper into situations and go past the obvious. It was all about asking questions while searching for the real meaning in events that are relevant to us all. There are so many unknown occurrences and issues in life. I felt that it was important to be better equipped to address those mysteries and come away with a few answers.

I opened my briefcase to retrieve my lesson plan, and class began.

CHAPTER 2

Time always seemed to fly when the class got into a good discussion. We were talking about the significant impact that, over time, various writings have had on our society. We agreed on the irony of the age-old truth that so often what a person says or does becomes famous only years after they die. We decided that while some speeches, writings, and philosophies impact society at the time of deliverance, they often escalate in popularity and influence after the author is deceased.

One student mentioned Lincoln's *Gettysburg Address* and its impact during the Civil War. She commented that Lincoln's sermon was the pebble, thrown into a pond, causing many rippling effects. Another brought up Dr. Martin Luther King Jr.'s famous speeches and how King's eloquence and actions had positively shaped the civil rights movement. I asked my students to think back even further in history. Someone in the back shouted out *Hammurabi's Code,* and another student pointed out *The Ten Commandments.* These writings outlined laws for our society, a way for people to live a life of order and harmony so that the righteous might rule and the wicked are destroyed. Without this foundation for written law, where would we be today?

One student, in the back of the room, raised her hand and asked, "What if parts of these famous writings had been left out or even lost over time? Would their impact have been diminished? What if Lincoln hadn't been called on to dedicate that cemetery during the Civil War, or if Martin Luther King Jr. hadn't spoken out on his beliefs? What if Hammurabi's Code initially contained 400 or 600 laws, rather than the 282 that are recorded? Or if there were really twelve, sixteen, or even twenty commandments, and we were missing out on those important writings?"

Someone else yelled out, "I'd fire the scribe!" I couldn't see who made the original comment, and time was about to run out, so I gave the homework assignment and dismissed the class.

Back in my office, I sat down and reached for my mail, but I didn't get too far. The first envelope stopped me dead in my tracks. It was made of old looking paper, had my name on it, and appeared to have been crumpled up before being sent to me. It looked just like the envelope I found on my kitchen table that morning, only slightly more wrinkled. I didn't remember this being in the stack of mail that I left behind before class, and there was no stamp or return address on it. As I opened the envelope, I noticed how warm it was in my office. It was still cool outside, and my window was partly open. How could it be warming up? Something felt odd, but I couldn't put my finger on it. I stood up to adjust the thermostat.

Inside the envelope was a piece of paper made from the same old, yellowish paper as the note I found on the kitchen table. The paper looked as if someone crumpled it before folding and placing the letter in the envelope. I unfolded the paper and read the following message:

The second ten exist. Trust your instincts.
Find Ayn in the old city. It
is time. You will see.

The note was exactly the same as the letter I read earlier in the morning, and the handwriting looked similar to that of my oldest daughter Sara. It didn't make any sense.

"What are 'the second ten?'" I asked myself aloud. *Who is Ayn, and what old city is it talking about? Did Sara write me a message in some sort of secret code? If it wasn't from her, where did this second note come from, and who is placing them about?* I continued thinking to myself.

Stupid joke, I thought.

I crumpled the note and envelope, tossed them in the trash, and finished reading my mail. The rest of the afternoon went according to routine. I did a little bit of research online, two students came by to ask a brief question, and I returned a few phone calls. The last thing I did before heading out was to review the next day's lesson plan and place it in my briefcase. I picked up my case and headed out the door toward my car.

The good part about Tuesdays was that they started at a leisurely pace. The bad part was that I drove home in traffic. My office hours went later on Tuesdays since I did not come in at all in the morning. I suppose that was the price I paid for being able to sleep in a little once a week. It seemed as if everything in life had a way of evening out.

Not bad philosophy for a history professor, I thought.

Jackie, Allison, and Sara were outside playing soccer when I finally pulled into the driveway.

If those girls played half as aggressively against their opponents as they did against each other, they would be incredible, I thought. Competition was definitely not lacking around our house.

Inside, Renee put the finishing touches on dinner, while Geoff hovered over his computer, engrossed in the latest *Build Your Own Civilization* game. It was actually rather quiet until the girls came thundering in. Allison dropped the ball on the floor and kicked it across the kitchen to Jackie. Jackie knocked it to Sara, who moved left, then right, then back to the left. She shot the ball past the large bay window and into a basket in the laundry room. SCORE!

They knew they weren't supposed to play ball in the house, but the action happened so quickly, and honestly I was quite impressed with their footwork, so I didn't say anything. The girls left the ball sitting idly in the laundry room and trampled back to the bathroom to wash up.

I went to the counter to check out the day's mail. Renee had already separated out the bills, and as usual, two out of every three pieces were catalogues or other junk. I made quick work of the stack, but I froze in my place when I saw the last piece of mail. I must have blinked twice before my mouth dropped so far open it could have hit the floor because Renee noticed and asked, "What's up?"

"This is just so strange," I said.

Then I recanted the day's happenings; first the letter on the kitchen table, then the letter at work, and now this.

The envelope had my name and address on it, but again, there was no stamp and no return address. I started to peel it open. The envelope was made of the same old-style parchment as the earlier letters, and it was even more creased. The envelope looked as if it had been balled up and stomped on before being sealed and placed in my stack of letters. The paper appeared in the same crumbled condition as the envelope.

These couldn't be the same..., I started thinking.

But I stopped that line of thought before I could take it too seriously. I unfolded the letter and started to read it. The message was eerily familiar.

The second ten exist. Trust your instincts.
Find Ayn in the old city. It
is time. You will see.

Although the words were now familiar, their meaning was still completely unclear. What did it mean? Where, or from whom, did it come? The first note was on smooth paper, and each subsequent letter arrived on increasingly more wrinkled paper.

This couldn't be the same envelope and letter I balled up and threw away twice today, could it? I thought.

The question scared me, and I was undoubtedly not equipped to deal with any of the possible explanations that were making their way into my head.

It was easier to just deal with the piece of paper, so I went into my bedroom and put the letter in my top nightstand drawer. It would be safe there, and if I didn't throw it away, it couldn't keep following me around.

CHAPTER 3

Wednesday morning began smoothly when I woke up at 5:30 for my early run. Renee and I saw the children off to school. With the four on their respective ways, Renee and I took a few minutes to grab some nourishment for the day before we had to head our separate ways. An article in the newspaper caught my eye as I was about to stand up from the kitchen table. A replica of the stone pillars containing Hammurabi's Code was coming to the Art Museum as part of a "Mesopotamian Legacy" exhibit at the museum.

That's funny, I thought, *one of my students just mentioned him yesterday. I'd love to see that this weekend. Maybe Geoff will want to come too.*

Before I could give it much more thought, I realized I was going to be late if I didn't leave soon, so I grabbed my briefcase by the back door and headed off to campus. The parking lot was packed this morning, but I managed to locate one of the few remaining spots in the faculty section. It was a short walk up the stairs, across the grassy quad, and into my building. On such a nice day I almost wished the distance would be longer between my car and my office. I was envious of the students who were relaxing on the quad. Some were tossing around a Frisbee or delving into a good book, while others were just lying there, sharing stories and soaking up the sun.

Sam, you would do anything to be outside, I thought as the door to Rosemont Hall swung open.

I taught two classes in the morning and then broke for lunch. There was a nice deli in the student union building next door, so I went there for a sandwich. I would choose this little deli over all of the fast food options any day, and buying something on campus was much more convenient than bringing a lunch from home. I never seemed to remember to bring food with me, so I often ended up at this café. I only had one more class to teach, and I wanted to catch up on my reading before it began, so I headed back to my office right after lunch. It was sunny out, and a few students were throwing a Frisbee around.

The life of college students, I thought. *The stresses sure do change when you are out of school and working.*

"Enjoy it while you can," I mumbled as I went into the building and up to my office.

The mail was on my desk, and I quickly went through it. There was a stack of magazines that I needed to take care of, so I picked up the first one, turned to the index, and looked for any interesting articles. There were two. I read both of them, tore out one that I conceived could be useful at some point, tossed the magazine in the recycle bin, and then picked up the next one. This procedure continued for some time as the stack of magazines slowly started to disappear.

About 2:15 in the afternoon there was a knock on the door. "Come in," I said, and in walked Dean Phillips.

"Hi Jack!" Jack Phillips had been the Dean of the School of Arts and Science since I came to Washington University as a graduate student. He has always been one of my biggest supporters. You had to admire a man like Jack. He was more than an educator or an administrator; Jack was a great leader. He always made it his business to know what you were working on and somehow found a way to give a hand here and a little help there. Everyone always rallied around Jack because we knew he had our best interests in mind.

Jack sat down.

"Sam, how's Renee doing?" he asked.

I told Jack about a few of the volunteer jobs Renee was involved in at both the middle and elementary schools, and Jack asked, "What's Renee going to do with her time when your kids go off to college?"

I said, "That's not going to be for a while, and I'm sure she'll find another cause to rally behind by then."

Jack forced a grin and nodded his head.

I could tell there was something on Jack's mind, so I asked, "What's up?"

Jack told me that Jay Stevens, another professor, had planned to participate in an international educators' conference next week while the school was on spring break. He was to leave tomorrow morning. Jay had been in a car accident and broke his right leg in two places. Traveling was out of the question.

"Is your passport current?" asked Jack. "I know it's short notice but do you think you could fill in and attend the meeting?"

I had a peculiar feeling that there was more to the story.

"Is that all?" I asked somewhat inquisitively.

"Well," said Jack with a prolonged pause. "Jay was supposed to give a speech to kick things off on Sunday."

"Let me make sure I understand this," I quipped. "I have to leave in less than twenty-four hours, and I have to prepare a speech!"

Jack was in trouble, and I knew it. I should have used the occasion to my benefit, maybe asked for a raise or extra vacation days, but I just couldn't take advantage of Jack like that.

Renee and I had planned to stay home over spring break and relax. It was to be a welcome change of routine. The kids' spring break was the following week, so we were going to have one whole week, at home, to ourselves. I knew she would be disappointed, and I should have just said "no," but this was Jack.

I just asked, "Where is the conference?"

Jack replied, "Jerusalem."

CHAPTER 4

Thursday morning I woke up early, put the final few items in my suitcase, and had breakfast. I was booked on American flight #4722 at 11:10 that morning. Renee and the children drove me to the airport to see me off. Jackie seemed the most affected by my sudden departure. She always hated it when I went out of town. I didn't like to see her saddened, but I have to admit, it felt good to know I would be missed.

We parked the car in the short-term parking lot. Geoff found one of those luggage carts and brought it over to put my suitcase on it. With the cart in tow, the six of us barely fit inside the little service elevator.

Overseas travel was never easy, and security was at its tightest. At the counter I was asked a series of questions and my passport was checked.

Better to get everything done here in St. Louis then to have to deal with it in New York, I thought.

As it turned out, the routine was repeated in New York anyway, but I didn't know that at the time.

As we walked toward security, Sara found another luggage cart and was pushing Allison and Jackie down the hall. They were trying to see how fast they could go and how much they could swerve. After they had two near-miss collisions, I called out to them to slow down. The last thing I wanted them to do was wipe out an unsuspecting bystander.

Dad was the bad guy again, I thought.

Before I went through security I kissed everyone goodbye. At the gate I checked to see if an emergency row seat was available. It wasn't and I boarded the airplane. The thought of the eighteen-hour trip through New York to Tel Aviv was not a pleasant one. It was a long enough trip when Renee was with me, and I wasn't looking forward to traveling alone. There was also the task of writing that speech.

Why couldn't Jay have at least have had his speech done already? I wished. *Then I could've just enjoyed the conference and given his speech without the stress of writing a new one.*

The airplane lifted off the runway and headed east. I looked out the window next to me at the deceptively miniature city I saw below. There were plenty of little houses and buildings, tiny cars filled the roads, and golf courses looked to be sized for 6-inch people. There below me was the wandering Mississippi River and the famous St. Louis Arch. Although the arch started and ended at the ground, it looked like a giant, endless, steel oval, half covered by dirt. It was as if this ring had been stuck in the ground, and only half of it was left exposed.

Endless steel, I thought to myself. A circle with no beginning, no end. History seemed endless, going on, with no end in sight. A continuum. And then it hit me. That's what I would talk about in my opening keynote. *Education, the endless search of humankind to learn from the past, but to teach for the future.* Endlessness, no start and no finish. Just being. Just experiencing. Just learning and growing. I grabbed my laptop and started pounding on the keys.

I wanted to have the speech done before I landed in Tel Aviv. I was scheduled to speak on Sunday, and if all went well, I would arrive on Friday with my speech in hand, and be able to spend Saturday relaxing on the beach. The thought of, within a few hours, being able to swim in the Mediterranean Sea was appealing. Maybe things were going to turn out well after all.

❊ ❊ ❊

In New York I had a couple of hours to kill before boarding my flight to Tel Aviv. I wished that I changed airplanes in Boston instead of New York. *At least there I can get a good meal in the airport at Legal Seafood,* I thought. Their chowder was the best, and I always enjoyed the great fish they served. Before long I was on board El Al Airlines flight #3022. We taxied to the end of the runway, picked up speed, and lifted off over the ocean. Next stop, Tel Aviv.

Shortly after takeoff, dinner was served. Experience had taught me to eat dinner at the airport in New York so I wouldn't have to subject myself to the airline food. The meal didn't look too bad though, so I picked at it.

I always eat too much when I travel. I'll go for a run when I get to Jerusalem, I reflected.

After a couple of hours, I dozed off. When I awoke, the airplane was completely dark, and most of the passengers were asleep. I took in a deep breath. There was no mistaking the dry, stale air of a commercial airliner. I turned on my reading light, a spotlight shining in the darkness of the airplane cabin, and I flipped open my computer to go over the speech. I just needed to come up with the closing story, and I would be done. I rummaged through my bag for the yellow file folder. Before I left St. Louis, I pulled a file that I kept various stories in from my desk. I thought they could come in handy for my speech. As I flipped through the folder, I came to a familiar piece of paper. It was the wrinkled parchment that I had thrown in my nightstand.

Renee must have thought I wanted it and threw it in the file, I told myself. I stuffed the piece of paper in my pocket and continued writing.

After a while I stopped writing and put my hand into my pocket to check on the paper. I pulled out the parchment and reread it. Written in perfect English on the paper were the following words:

> *The second ten exist. Trust your instincts.*
> *Find Ayn in the old city. It*
> *is time. You will see.*

I still didn't understand what this encrypted note meant, and I just couldn't comprehend how it kept showing up. I shoved it back in my pocket, finished my speech, and then shut my eyes for a little rest.

CHAPTER 5

My flight landed in Tel Aviv at 10:35 in the morning. Right on time. The conference started Sunday afternoon, so I had two days to take it easy and practice my speech. I gathered my luggage and went to the Hertz counter to pick up my rental car. I had a hotel reservation 50 kilometers from the airport at a Sheraton in Jerusalem, where our conference was being held.

I'm glad Dad taught me to drive a standard transmission, I thought.

Every time I travel overseas it seems like the only car left on the lot has a manual shift. But it was no problem, so I took a map and headed out of the rental car lot. One road from the airport went west to downtown Tel Aviv. I went to the right and turned east toward Jerusalem.

Spring must be the best time to visit Israel. It was a beautiful, sunny day, and as the road twisted upward toward Jerusalem, the hillsides were ablaze with flowers. The terraced hillsides of olive groves and grapevines had such a biblical charm.

Jerusalem is a magnificent city, really two cities in one. The old city, surrounded by its majestic walls, and the new city containing new structures, government buildings, and new residential areas. It's a special place. I love the fact that it is sacred to three religions. The historical sites include monuments and shrines for Jews, Christians, and Muslims. Unfortunately, it's also a hotbed of discontent, but I don't stop hoping that will eventually change. Maybe one day Jerusalem will be a model city; a place where all people from many diverse backgrounds will learn to live together with respect and care.

Before I knew it, I was pulling into the Sheraton. I dropped off the car, walked inside to check in, and went up to my room. It only took a few minutes to unpack. I hung up the suit that I would be wearing for my speech so it would look nice, took a quick shower to wash away the fatigue from the long trip, and headed downstairs to find something to eat. I was starving!

I knew I wanted falafel for lunch. I just love that fresh pita bread, filled with deep fried balls of crushed chickpeas, a few slices of cucumber, some tomato, and a pickle slice. The white sesame sauce tops it off perfectly. What a real treat! Falafel in Israel is like hot dogs in New York City, there are street vendors selling it all over the place. Each vendor puts their own little twist on the traditional Middle Eastern staple. On previous trips to Israel I lived off of falafel, eating them several times a day. I surmised that this trip would be no different.

I went up to the bellman at the front of the hotel and asked him to direct me to the closest falafel stand. With a thick Israeli accent, the bellman asked me, "Do you want the closest, or the best falafel?"

After a pause and a quick thought, I said, "The best." I had time. *Why not do it right?* I thought.

The bellman said there was an old man nearby who made the best falafel in all of Jerusalem. I was directed out the front door and to the left. A few blocks down would be Sholmtzion Street, and the stand on the corner was the one to go to. I asked the bellman how I would know which was the right one.

He responded, "The old man's name is Ayn."

All of a sudden it was as if everything around me stood still. I stopped in my tracks and reached in my pocket. There was the crumpled piece of old paper. I reread the words, even though by now I knew them by heart.

The second ten exist. Trust your instincts.
Find Ayn in the old city. It
is time. You will see.

I walked out the door and headed down the street. *Who is the Ayn it is talking about?* I thought. Surely it couldn't be this old street vendor I was walking toward. *Was the old city referring to Jerusalem?* I wondered. "Sure, my destiny was to come to Jerusalem and meet this old falafel vendor so he could change my life," I finally surmised with a sarcastic chuckle. This was all getting a little bit too bizarre.

I walked past Independence Park and crossed the street to the far corner. There was a small wagon with a sign overhead and an old man standing right behind. I walked up and said, "The bellman at the Sheraton said that Ayn made the best falafel in town. Are you Ayn?" I didn't even know if he spoke English. The man looked me over from my head down to my feet and back to my eyes.

He said, "I am, and your bellman is correct."

I ordered one falafel, and Ayn begin cutting the pita open. I watched as his old hands worked surely and deliberately. *He must have done this a million times,* I thought.

"What brings you to Israel?" he asked without looking away from the food in front of him.

I was tempted to say, "An airplane," but he might not understand my humor, and I thought that would be rude. "I'm giving a speech at the International Education Conference on Sunday," I said.

"You must have something important to say like Socrates at the Acropolis or your former President Lincoln at Gettysburg," Ayn responded. It caught me off guard, and I was actually sort of surprised that this street merchant was so educated. "Actually, I'm filling in for one of my friends," I said.

"Well, maybe it was meant to be that you are here. Perhaps your message is really what everyone needs," Ayn said.

He handed me the completed falafel, and as his hand approached mine I felt a sudden wave of heat. *It must be the falafel,* I thought. "Toda raba," thank you in Hebrew, I blurted out. That was almost the extent of my conversational Hebrew.

"Bavakasha," you're welcome, responded Ayn.

I took a bite. Maybe I was just hungry. Maybe it had been a while since I had last eaten falafel. Or, maybe the bellman was just right, and this was the best falafel in town.

Seeing my satisfaction, Ayn smiled with a sense of accomplishment. He then asked, "What will you speak about on Sunday?"

"Learning from our past, using that information to plan for our future, and how we can create the future we desire based on the choices we make," I said.

"The past can be a powerful teacher," said Ayn. "The only problem is that, sometimes, history is not accurately recorded. We don't have all the lessons from our past that we should. Sometimes we even forget some of the lessons that have been taught us," Ayn said, showing some concern.

Pretty deep thoughts for a street vendor, I thought to myself.

"With all the history and philosophy that has been recorded through the ages and then passed down, generation to generation, don't you think it's possible that some messages were never recorded or that some books or scrolls were lost?" asked Ayn.

All of a sudden I was hearing the same words spoken at the end of my class on Tuesday. It sounded just like the comments made by that unknown student obscured in the back of my classroom. It still seemed like an interesting point, but this man was a simple vendor on a street corner in Israel, and his increasing fanaticism caught me slightly by surprise.

I was, however, enjoying our conversation; but nevertheless, I wanted to get back to the hotel and finish working on my speech. If I were sufficiently prepared today, I could spend some time tomorrow on the beach in Tel Aviv. A just reward, I felt. I bid Ayn goodbye and started to walk off, but he was still in midstream of an idea. As I turned to leave he asked me a question.

"What if there weren't ten commandments, as our world believes? What if there were more?" asked Ayn.

I was taking a bite of my falafel and stepping off the curb to cross the street when his words hit my ears. His comment totally took me by surprise. I was so caught up in his statement that I didn't notice anything happening around me. The next thing I heard was a loud bus horn. I looked up to see a city bus bearing down on me. I had been so caught up in Ayn's words that I didn't pay proper attention as I stepped off the curb. Just as I was about to be hit, I felt a flash of heat and a strong grip pull me back up onto the sidewalk.

When I caught my breath, and turned around, Ayn was standing right behind me. A moment ago he was behind his falafel stand. How did he move that fast? Where did a man of his age get the strength to literally pull me out of harm's way? I was really baffled.

Ayn looked me straight in the eye and said, "The time is right. Go to your hotel and finish preparing your speech. Tomorrow is the Sabbath. Rest. I will as well. Come back Sunday after your speech and tell me how it went. I have a few ideas I want to ask you about."

I warily thanked Ayn for his bravery and very cautiously headed toward my hotel. Many of Ayn's words still stirred in my head. What did he want to ask me on Sunday? What did he mean, "The time is right?" Did he mean it was time for me to go to the hotel or was it time for something else? *Time,* I thought. Then I pulled out the crumpled piece of paper once more.

The second ten exist. Trust your instincts.
Find Ayn in the old city. It
is time. You will see.

These words kept showing up. Over and over again the content of this message was being pushed in front of my face. I wondered, *What does it mean? Why me? What's going on?!*

I walked back to the hotel with all of these unanswered questions swirling around in my head.

I spent the balance of Friday afternoon putting the finishing touches on my speech. Admittedly, it was very difficult to concentrate on my speech with the whole event at the falafel stand still consuming my mind. His words almost matched identically the discussion in my class on Tuesday. His name was the same as on the mysterious note. He mentioned, "The time is right," and the note said, "It is time." He spoke of the concept of twenty commandments instead of the ten that we all know about. I pondered, *Are there possibly ten additional commandments that were somehow lost? Could those ten additional command-ments be the "other ten" that the note mentioned?*

Friday at sunset Israel literally shuts down. All the stores and restaurants close up with the onset of the Sabbath. I ate dinner in the hotel and decided to get to bed early. I was exhausted from the long trip and I was nowhere near to adjusting for the time change. *Tomorrow I'll take it easy,* I thought as I drifted off to sleep.

CHAPTER 6

I awoke early the next morning and opened my eyes for a brief moment before I rolled over and went back to sleep. Finally I decided to get up and go out for a little exercise. I always enjoy going for a run when I travel. It's a great way to see a new city from a different perspective. As I ran through the city streets of Jerusalem, I passed all sorts of people. Some were walking to Shabbat services with family members, while others were out for a quiet walk around the neighborhood. The air was clear, and it was a great time to run.

I came back from my excursion and took a quick shower. I got dressed, grabbed a small duffel bag, threw a towel in it, and headed downstairs. I had a traditional Israeli breakfast of hard-boiled eggs, cucumber slices, fresh bread, and a glass of juice. I asked the doorman to call for my car, and I headed out of Jerusalem, west, toward Tel Aviv.

I decided to park at the Hilton Hotel so I could use their beach, and within an hour I was looking at the Mediterranean Sea. Its deep blue water contrasted beautifully with the sun-bleached white sand. It was a windy day, and the ocean was filled with waves. Small white caps appeared on top of the waves as they fell forward and worked their way to the shore.

Bathers filled the area close to the shoreline. It was a little cool, and it seemed as if they didn't want to get too deep into the water. Farther out, schools of sailboards were dancing about. The wind was perfect for sailing, and the ocean became a playground of sailboarders working their boards back and forth along the beach. Every now and then someone would direct their board directly into a wave and jump into the air.

Talented people make difficult things look easy, I thought.

I laid on the sand for a while before going into the water, just relaxing and taking in the comfortable warmth of the sun. There was a modest crowd on the beach, and it was great fun watching all the people involved in their individual activities. Eventually, I got up and enjoyed the feel of the cool water splashing against me as the tide came in and out. After a few minutes, I went back to my towel and laid down. I wanted to feel the full warmth of the sun. Still not fully adapted to the time change, I quickly closed my eyes and began to dose off.

The warmth of the sun felt good, but suddenly it disappeared, leaving a patch of shade above me. I opened my eyes to find a man standing over me, blocking out the sun. At first my eyes weren't adjusted, and I didn't recognize the old man. Then I realized who was standing over me. It was Ayn.

"I thought the beach would be a nice place to visit today," he said as he sat down to join me.

I hadn't invited him, but it seems as if older people sometimes just take charge and do as they please. Anyway, I liked Ayn and welcomed his company. Besides, I still had so many unanswered questions. So much mystery surrounded this entire trip.

"It's a wonderful day to rest and enjoy the world around us, isn't it?" asked Ayn.

"Were you looking for me?" I replied.

"I thought you might be here," Ayn said.

Of all the places in Israel, why did he think I would be here? I asked myself.

"Are you ready for your speech tomorrow?" he asked, nonchalantly changing the subject.

I proceeded to tell him about my speech, the points I wanted to make, and the conclusion I would present. Ayn seemed impressed.

"Sounds well thought out," he said.

Over the next hour Ayn proceeded to ask about my family, my job, how I felt about the state of affairs of the world, and the tremendous unrest existing in such a holy city like Jerusalem. It was as if he was trying to get inside my head. He continued to probe me with questions, as if he was searching for deeper thoughts on a score of issues. I felt as if I was at a job interview.

Yesterday's conversation and events at the falafel stand were still swirling in my head. I had questions that *I* wanted to ask Ayn, but I never had the chance.

All of a sudden Ayn said, "Well, I have to go. Good luck with your speech tomorrow, and come by for a falafel afterward. It's on me!"

I bid him goodbye, and he strolled down the beach. He crossed over a stone barrier and was gone.

I packed up my things and started to walk to my car. I wanted to get back to Jerusalem, take a shower, and go to dinner. I had just the place in mind.

CHAPTER 7

Jerusalem comes to life after sunset on Saturday. It's as if the entire city is trying to make up for twenty-four hours of inactivity in just one evening. The streets buzz with cars and people throughout the festive night. I decided to head to Ben Yehuda Street. On Saturday evenings people come to stroll and browse in the stores while the popular avenue is closed to cars, and the street is lined with one cafe after another. It seems like a giant outdoor party, and the entire city is invited. After looking in a few windows, I found a sidewalk cafe that looked nice enough and sat down at a table. I wanted to eat dinner, review my speech in my mind, and then get a good night's sleep.

I ordered a plate of humus and some pitas. I tore off a piece of pita and dipped it in the chickpea mixture. There was plenty of garlic in the humus, and it was great. For dinner I had broiled chicken and some of the best french fries I have ever eaten. It was a feast!

As I ate, I tried to review my upcoming speech, but I just couldn't concentrate. My thoughts kept returning to the mysterious note, the conversation with Ayn at the falafel stand, and our "chance" meeting on the beach earlier that day. I felt that the course of events during the past few days were somehow arranged, and that I was not in control of everything that had transpired. I thought of the strange note, Jay Stevens' car accident, the resulting trip to Jerusalem, and Ayn at the falafel stand and then on the beach.

Where is all this heading? Why these events? And why me? I wondered. And then, the inevitable question, *What will be the outcome of all these occurrences?*

After I finished eating, I decided to walk off dinner. *Maybe I can find a gift for Renee,* I thought. I knew just what I wanted, and I looked in several stores until I found the item. The shofar was incredibly large. The traditional ram's horn trumpet went around and around like a corkscrew and for almost three feet, and there was also a Lucite stand to place it on.

"Wow! Renee would love to place this on our mantel," I said to myself.

I had the shofar and the stand packed very carefully, because I knew it had to travel a long way. The box was placed in a shopping bag, and I walked out of the store. I picked up a few items for the kids and started to head back. It was a short walk back up King George V to my hotel, and I was feeling good about the gift I found for Renee. I couldn't wait to see the look on her face when she unwrapped it.

I walked into the Sheraton, checked the front desk for messages, and went upstairs.

One last time through my speech, and I'll be ready for tomorrow, I thought.

Before I went to bed I wanted to call home. It would be late Saturday afternoon in St. Louis, and I might be lucky and catch someone at home. The phone rang three times.

One more ring and I'll get the answering machine, I thought.

It was times like these when I didn't want to leave a message. All I wanted to do was talk to Renee or one of the kids!

Before the phone could ring a fourth time, someone picked it up. It was Jackie. Just hearing her voice made me feel good. I knew that both she and

Allison had soccer tournaments over the weekend, and I wondered how they were doing.

"We're doing okay," Jackie said. "We're one and one, and I scored twice."

"Good! I wish I could have been there," I replied. "How is Alli's team doing?"

"They won both games and Al scored once."

A victory Sunday would guarantee a spot in the finals for both teams.

Geoff was out playing tennis, and Sara was on the computer, but she came to the phone when she heard it was me. I also talked to Renee. She sounded fine, and told me to have fun when I gave my speech the next day.

"That's easy for you to say," I told her, but deep down I knew she was right. If I have fun, my audience will also have fun, I reminded myself.

I fought to clear my head and forced myself to go through my speech one last time. I crawled into bed and turned out the lights. A good night's sleep was more than welcome before the morning's big event. Besides, I had some unanswered questions that I was intent on getting to the bottom of. I was going to take Ayn up on his offer for lunch—and get some answers at the same time.

CHAPTER 8

The sun blasted through the window early the next morning. In my haste to get to bed, I hadn't completely closed the curtains. I was paying the price with an early wake-up call, but the warmth of the sun felt good on my face.

I took a shower, got dressed, and went downstairs for breakfast. I continued to think through some details of my speech as I slipped behind the steering wheel and drove away from the hotel. It was a quick drive to Hebrew University. My speech was at 9, but I wanted to arrive early and check out the sound system. With any luck I would give my speech, shake a few hands at the following reception, and be out of there by 11:30.

At 8:10 I parked my car and went into the large auditorium. The auditorium could hold 1,500 people, and I was told it would be full. I swallowed hard.

No time to get nervous, I thought in vain.

I asked for my microphone and checked it out. The sound quality was great, and the volume was perfect. Now all I had to do was distract myself for the next forty minutes. If I thought about the speech too much, I knew that I would be a basket case by 9. Images of Ayn kept flooding into my mind, and it was evident that I had to get some answers to my questions. As soon as my speech was over, I would get to the bottom of the mysterious note and this Ayn guy once and for all. For now though, I needed to push this out of my mind completely so that I was not thoroughly preoccupied throughout my discourse.

The auditorium filled to capacity, and I was introduced. I walked out on stage and began my presentation. After a couple of humorous stories about the children and some rather unusual marathon experiences, I zeroed in on my core message, learning from the past and teaching for the future. I was almost done when I saw an older man toward the back of the room get up to walk out. He looked strangely familiar.

Is that Ayn? I wondered. *It couldn't be,* I reasoned. The room was dim, and it was hard to make out his features. As I stared intently at this figure, I stumbled on a couple of words before I quickly regained my composure, and then went on. When I looked back, the man was gone.

The speech ended, the crowd applauded, and I walked off the stage. Whew! I was glad that was done. I hung around to talk with some of the attendees, shook a few congratulatory hands, and had a glass of water.

Although I knew that I should stay and take in a few of the smaller meetings, Ayn was all I could think about. First it was the letter that wouldn't go away, and now this guy kept popping up. Ayn owned the falafel stand, showed up on the beach, and might have been at my speech.

He's everywhere!

This was too much. I needed answers. I went to get them.

CHAPTER 9

I dropped off my car with the bellman at the front door, went upstairs, and changed out of my suit. I slipped on my black polo shirt, new khakis, and favorite Ecco shoes. I wanted to be comfortable. As I stood in the hallway, it seemed like the elevator took forever to arrive, but finally the doors opened, and I walked into the crowded space. It didn't stop at all after my floor as we sped down toward the lobby. Again, the doors opened. I walked out of the cramped elevator, across the hotel lobby, and through the revolving doors.

I headed across the front yard of the hotel and left toward the main road. It was only a few short blocks to Sholmtzion Street and the corner where Ayn worked at his falafel stand. Three people were getting food when I approached. They paid their money, were handed what they ordered, and then walked off. I was left alone with Ayn.

"How was your speech?" Ayn asked as he straightened up his cart.

"I thought I saw you in the back of the room," I responded.

Ayn didn't acknowledge my comment as he continued to wipe off the small counter. He didn't even look up, but asked, "Did you get the response you desired?"

"Yes," I said, "the audience reacted as I hoped, but you are not. I need some answers."

"What kind of answers are you seeking from me?" asked Ayn. "You are the teacher."

I produced the old paper note that I had kept in my pocket. "Know anything about this?" I asked as I passed the piece of paper to Ayn.

"Interesting," was all he muttered before asking, "Do you know where it's from?"

"I was hoping you knew," I responded. "I am thoroughly perplexed. There have been many coincidences. First this note, then my last minute need to come to Israel for my speech, and finally you and your falafel stand."

Ayn looked at me in silence, and then asked, "Do you have a car?"

"Yes, I rented one," I said.

"Good. Get it and be back here in twenty minutes. I'll clean up the stand and put it away. We'll go for a little drive and see if we can find your answers," Ayn said.

Then, before I could open my mouth to object or ask another question, Ayn turned and started to push his cart down the street. He didn't look back once, as he rounded the next corner and disappeared.

I walked back to the hotel and had my car brought around. I couldn't believe that I was actually going along with this guy.

Where were we going? I wondered. *Why couldn't Ayn just tell me what I wanted to know? Am I putting myself in danger by going with this stranger?*

He seemed kind and gentle, and he did pull me from in front of that bus the other day, but I still wasn't sure.

Twenty minutes had passed and I was back at Ayn's corner in the car. He wore old blue jeans, a T-shirt, and a light jacket. When I stopped, he opened the door, slid into the seat next to me, and said, "Go that way," as he pointed his finger straight ahead.

We drove for a few minutes before he said, "Turn right."

We turned onto Highway 1 and headed east out of Jerusalem. After driving in silence for about forty-five minutes, I finally broke down and asked, "Are we driving all the way to Jordan?"

Ayn didn't answer, but after a few more minutes he said to turn right, so I turned south onto Highway 90. The sun was low on the horizon and shinning directly into my right eyes as I drove.

It wasn't long before I saw water off to my left. I realized it was the Dead Sea. The sun was setting and we drove farther and farther away from civilization. We passed the oasis of Ein Gedi. I remembered an earlier trip to Israel when we hiked up a trail along the stream back to a waterfall and natural swimming hole. It was a lush green oasis in the middle of an otherwise barren desert.

Somehow I don't think we're going to end up at an oasis, I thought.

Another thirty minutes passed before Ayn motioned to the right.

"But there's no road," I observed.

Ayn said, "Slow down and turn right up ahead."

About one hundred feet passed and then there was an old dirt road on my right. I came to a complete stop in the middle of the road and looked at Ayn.

"We can't go there," I groaned.

"We can, we must, and we will," Ayn replied.

I turned right and began down the road. The car bumped along, and I could feel every rut and rock in the road. As we drove through the desert, all I could see was sand, rock, and sky as they blurred together.

"I'm glad I took out the extra insurance when I rented the car," I said to Ayn, almost jokingly.

He didn't respond.

Great, I'm going to have to call Hertz and have them retrieve the car from the middle of the desert, I thought.

By now the sun was down and the only light was the illuminating stream from the car's headlights. I expected a boulder to jump out at us at any moment. With the lack of sunshine, the temperature was dropping. I rolled up my window to keep the heat in and the dust of the dirt road out. Ayn did the same.

I didn't feel good about this. It was night, we were in the middle of nowhere, and we just kept moving farther and farther away from what I thought was safety. I thought that I had really made a mistake in trusting this old man.

Where are my senses? I asked myself. *I have a wife and four children, and I'm out in the middle of nowhere with someone I just met. I'm going to be robbed and my car will be stolen for sure.*

I just kept driving down the old dirt road. Suddenly rock walls appeared on both sides of the car, and it became evident we were driving into a canyon.

CHAPTER 10

The old dirt road continued deeper and deeper into the canyon. The canyon walls went straight up on either side of the car, and I noticed them drawing closer and closer. The canyon was narrowing and we were running out of room. As we rounded the bend, a dead end seemingly jumped out in front of us. There was nowhere left to go. It was so narrow we couldn't even turn the car around.

Great. I followed this old man right into the middle of nowhere, and now I can't even turn around and go home, I thought.

Just when I figured that I would be backing the car all the way out, Ayn said, "We're here!"

Where's here? I wondered.

There was just enough room to open the doors and squeeze out of the car. The canyon walls were almost vertical. The light of the full moon danced off of the rock walls and cast interesting shadows on the canyon floor. If you let your imagination run wild, those shadows took on the shapes of different animals.

Look up gullible in the dictionary, and you will find my name, I mused.

Ayn said, "Come on."

"It's a dead end. Where are we going?" I asked.

"Up. See that ledge up there?" Ayn said as he pointed up into the darkness. "That is where we need to be."

I looked up. All I saw was rock, steep rock. The moonlight played tricks on my eyes. The shadows cast from the rocks made the face of the wall almost impossible to fully figure out.

"Where's the ladder?" I asked, knowing that I did not really want to hear the answer.

"There is no ladder. We will climb," stated Ayn.

"How are we going to climb? It's dark. I'm not a climber. I have no experience in this. We could get seriously hurt, or worse!"

"Just follow me," responded Ayn. "I know how to go. Put your hands where I put my hands. Put your feet where I put my feet. Walk in my footsteps. If I get too far out of sight, then follow your instincts. After you have followed me for a while, your instincts will improve, you will know what is right and be comfortable acting on that judgment."

"But what about all those rocks?" I asked. "How are we going to climb over them and get up this wall?"

"There are lots of rocks sticking out of the canyon's side," Ayn acknowledged.

Like everyday events in our lives, we can see these rocks as obstacles, as barriers to our success. We can let the rock secure our failure. We can allow the rocks to keep us from our destiny. Or, we can use the rocks to our advantage. The rocks become handholds and small ledges on which we can place our feet. The rocks become the ladder to our goal, and help secure our success.

We started up the rock wall at the end of the canyon. I tried to look up ahead, to see the ledge we were climbing toward, but it was out of sight. I realized that the only way I was going to reach that ledge, and even just to survive, was not to look way out into the dark but to focus on what was going on right in front of me. I needed to focus on the now. I needed to be acutely aware of what was happening right at this exact moment in time.

What was Ayn doing? Where was he going? What was going to be my next hand hold? All these thoughts flooded into my mind.

Step-by-step, rock-by-rock, and inch-by-inch we worked our way up the rock wall. There was no clear path, yet each time I moved forward, another small rock to hold on to presented itself. A place that I could position my foot and push upward appeared each time. Occasionally a larger rock to rest on would arise. Opportunities naturally came to me as we journeyed up the canyon wall.

I realized that climbing this wall was very much like life. We start on a journey and don't always know the destination, or maybe we know where we're heading but just not exactly how to get there. As time passes and we continue to make efforts to grow and move forward, ideas and solutions naturally present themselves. Climbing this wall was very similar.

We climbed and climbed. I lost all track of time, and I could no longer see the bottom of the canyon. It was still completely dark ahead of me, but the space between my body and the floor was also filled with darkness. I realized that there was no way to turn back. Going down was not an option. I could only go forward. We climbed for so long that I started to wonder, *Why didn't we just come down from the top?*

Having someone to follow made climbing easier. I encouraged my students to find someone successful, someone who has accomplished what it is the student wants to accomplish, to help show the way. In this same manner, Ayn was my guide on this difficult climb. I kept wondering how was a person of Ayn's age able to climb so effortlessly. I was in great shape and still had trouble keeping up.

I checked to see where Ayn was and realized he was out of sight. Fear raced through my heart, but I remembered what he had said, "Trust your instincts." I kept reaching for the next hold and pushing up with my legs. Slowly I continued moving up the face of the wall.

I climbed over a big rock and realized that I was at the base of the ledge. Ayn must have already reached it. I put my right hand onto the ledge and pushed with my left foot. The rock under my foot gave way, and I started to lose my grip! I couldn't hold my entire weight with just one hand. I knew that I was going to fall, and the only thing between me and the bottom of the canyon was hundreds of sharp rocks.

As my mind began to race and flashes appeared before my eyes, I suddenly felt a strong pull on the collar of my shirt. In one swift movement I was pulled up and placed on top of the ledge. I looked up and into Ayn's eyes. I could see the care and concern he had for me.

"Thank you," were my only words. I sat for a moment as I attempted to catch my breath.

"That was not easy, Ayn," I stated as I stood up.

I thought about everything that had just happened and realized that I probably had learned more climbing that cliff than I had learned in a long time. Ayn was one living lesson after another. When I was with him, I felt more like the student than the teacher. Actually, I felt like I was the child and Ayn was the parent. Ayn combined knowledge, care, concern, and a never-ending stream of lessons. It felt good to be in his presence. As much as I enjoyed all of the learning, I still wondered where this was all going.

"All your answers are in there," Ayn said as he pointed toward the rock face in front of us.

I looked up and saw a small opening in the wall in front of me. It was a cave. The opening was covered with spider webs, which seemingly sealed the opening and guarded the entrance. I wasn't thrilled at the thought of going through those webs and into the unknown, but Ayn pushed through the webs, so I followed. He reached down, picked up a stick, and struck a match. The torch came alive and filled the small cave with a warm glow.

We were both bent over a bit as we started walking. As I followed, my plethora of questions kept darting around inside my head. I could not dwell on them for long, though, before I was distracted by a musty odor that filled my nose. Everything about this cave seemed old.

Ayn was as focused as I had ever seen him. After several minutes we walked into a larger chamber. The ceiling was high enough so we could stand fully erect. It felt great to straighten my back. There were four tunnels leading off of this larger chamber. Ayn looked up and went directly to the second tunnel from the left. I followed. Within a few moments we came to a branch in the tunnel and went to the right. It was then that it hit me.

How are we going to find our way out of here? I wondered. Maybe Hansel and Gretel's way was best, but I didn't have any bread to leave a trail. Ayn did not seem concerned, and I was not about to interrupt him. Not only was he completely focused, but also Ayn wore a look of complete determination.

He moved forward with an ever-growing conviction and determination. After about thirty minutes, the tunnel widened and finally opened up into a large room.

It was the end of the line.

CHAPTER 11

The first thing I noticed as we entered this chamber was that there was light. Before, there had been virtually no illumination; however, now I looked up to see light coming in from above. A single beam radiated down on us. It flowed into the room from the center of the ceiling and shone down at an angle toward the back wall. Was it sunlight coming in through a crack in the rock ceiling? I couldn't tell what the source of this light was. It was just there. As we approached the section of wall where the light hit the rock, I could make out some carvings in the stone. I saw an abundance of decorative symbols, and there were a couple of shoddy shelves cut into the wall...at least they looked like they were *supposed* to be shelves, but I wasn't really sure. The ones on the left were empty, but on the right, the poorly constructed shelves had something sitting on them.

Ayn reached up to retrieve what was on the top shelf.

He said, "This is what we came for. Here are the answers to your many questions."

Ayn lifted a large scroll and placed it on top of a large flat rock in front of him. The rock was waist high, about six feet square, and caught some of the light coming from above. Ayn motioned toward the floor and said, "There is some paper over there. Bring it here."

I went toward the wall and out of the light's path. I could vaguely make out a pile of something lying on the ground a few feet away. The paper felt old and brittle in my fingers. I set the stack down on the rock table Ayn was standing next to.

"What's all this?" I asked. "What is this cave, and what do all these carvings on the wall mean? Is something missing from that empty shelf? Are we too late? Did someone take something from here? What is that scroll you placed on the rock?"

I couldn't hold back anymore. Question after question raced from my brain to my mouth and flowed out into the emptiness of the cave. Only after I stopped to take a deep breath of air did Ayn finally respond.

"I'll tell you what you need to know to do your job," he said. Then Ayn asked, "Do you ever play games at home with your children?"

"We play them all the time," I answered, thinking of the closets filled with puzzles and board games that Renee and I play with the four kids.

"Why do you play them?" Ayn questioned.

"Well, we like to be together as a family. It's a great way to create a sense of family unity and bond with one another. We have fun, and everyone is very competitive," I responded.

"How do you know how to play those games?" Ayn asked.

"We read the rules," I stated matter-of-factly. I felt as if he was trying to make a point, but I just couldn't see where he was going with this line of questioning.

Everyone knows you have to read the rules of the game if you want to know how to play. Why is he asking me these questions? I thought to myself.

"What would happen if a game you bought was missing half of the rules? Isn't the purpose of the game to maximize your results based on your ability to apply the rules to your given situation?" Ayn quizzed.

"If we wanted to play bad enough, we would have to improvise. We would make up the necessary rules to complete the game. The kids are pretty creative and when they are determined to make something happen, we are usually able to salvage the situation and have a good time," I said.

Then Ayn asked, "But the original rules were probably well thought out, proven over time, and designed to allow you to create the best experience, weren't they?"

"Yes," I answered, still wondering where he was going with this line of questioning. Just then he unloaded the answer I was looking for, but not expecting.

"People have been playing the game of life with improvised rules. They were given a magnificent set of rules by which to play; however, it is as if they threw away pages three and four from the instruction pamphlet. Contained in this scroll are one half of the laws people need to create happiness and significance in their lives. The principles that these laws teach have been completely missing in many of our lives, because we have been improvising for all these years. As we established before, the rules that we make up cannot be as well thought out and successful as the intended guidelines."

"Great," I said cynically. "I've come all this way, and I only get half of the solution."

Ayn stared straight into my eyes and calmly said, "You already have the first Ten Commandments. These are the lost commandments."

Silence fell in the chamber. I could feel the tension building until it was so thick that it was hard to breathe. I didn't know what to think much less say. Unsure of how serious I should take Ayn, I asked, "What lost commandments?"

Ayn then responded with the whole story. "People of the world live by many rules and laws. For the most part they are based on a set of old teachings. Society calls those teachings *The Ten Commandments*. The truth of the matter is that there were more than ten commandments when they were originally written. There were twenty fundamental, guiding principles. Half of them were lost over time. The missing ten complete the story and give people everything they need to be rich beyond imagination. Not only rich in material possessions, but also rich in spirit and rich in their relationships with all the peoples of the world.

"The richness you achieve will allow you to go beyond monetary needs. By studying, learning, and living your life based on these principles, these lost commandments, you will transcend the all-encompassing need to measure greatness in monetary terms and enable yourself to seek fulfillment in your life based on personal growth, the expansion of your mind, and contributing to the growth of others around you."

Silence again returned to the cave.

Is this guy for real? I thought. "How did you find these? Why now? Why me?" I asked, still slightly perplexed by the ambiguity that surrounded Ayn.

"I have chosen you. I decided to share this knowledge with you because you teach. You will learn these commandments, then you will share them with the world. The people of the world need these now more than ever. I thought that they might be able to use the Ten Commandments and figure out the rest, but that hasn't worked. If you live a life filled with these commands, you will not only be closer to your God, but you will also be able to achieve success and happiness on your own, through your own endeavors, without others setting expectations for you.

"These commandments will help you connect to the power that already resides within you, but is unutilized. Everything you ever dreamed of, and much you never thought possible, will be yours to enjoy. I want to share these lost commandments with you. The only thing I ask is that you take notes as you study with me, and when you return to your university, you teach, write, and share these commandments with the world."

Curiosity seeped into my head. "What is the first commandment?" I asked.

"First you must promise. You must promise that you will take what I teach you and share that knowledge with everyone you come in contact with," Ayn demanded in a warm and sincere tone.

"How can I make promises about something that I don't even know what it is?" I asked.

"You must first learn to trust," Ayn answered without hesitation.

Ayn looked straight at me. His eyes were seemingly connected to mine. I couldn't blink. I couldn't shut my eyes. I couldn't turn away. As his stare affixed to mine, no words were spoken. I felt my heart pounding in my chest. I thought I could even hear Ayn's heart beating. Then I realized that

I was not *hearing* his heartbeat, I could *feel* Ayn's heart beating in his chest. I could feel his calmness, warmth, and then suddenly, I felt trust.

There were no more questions about why or how. There were no more questions about what was going on. This was right. This was good. And for the first time, I knew that this had to be.

Malkhut...Sovereignty.
Thou shalt share thyself
with others by expressing
your authentic emotions
and thoughts.

CHAPTER 12

Ayn unrolled the scroll and read:

*"**Malkhut**... Sovereignty.*
Thou shalt share thyself with
others by expressing your authentic
emotions and thoughts."

"What does that mean?" I asked.

"You tell me," he responded, like any good teacher would.

"I feel like it means that I have to let others into my life."

"By revealing your goals, desires, and inner thoughts," Ayn added. "It also relates to the importance of being honest and upfront with others. We have to go out of our way to share with others what is important to us. It is not enough to simply respond when asked a question. Instead, we must search for the questions and answer them before they are asked.

"And you must be real, genuine, and unpretentious. Ultimately, we must be authentic. Those are hard traits to master, and most people don't. People are always sharing, but only for their personal gain. Or, they share information to boost their ego. Boosting your ego artificially makes you feel important. You cannot be sovereign over, or fully control and enjoy your life until you are truly authentic with yourself and with others," Ayn said.

I nodded my head in agreement.

"This makes sense to you, doesn't it? You got this one really fast."

"I understand the words, but I don't really see the great significance that makes them commandment-worthy."

"The significance?! The significance is monumental," Ayn said with a hint of frustration in his voice.

We went on to discuss the concept in great detail, examining it from different angles. Together we decided that unless we truly share our lives with the important people who surround us, we would miss out on a substantial part of life.

"Like love and heartbreak, birth and death, secrets and stories. There is so much going on in each one of our lives, it would be a tragedy to keep it all to ourselves. Sometimes it is hard to express our emotions and let the people in our lives know how we feel, but it is so important. Too often we assume that our loved ones know how we feel about them, but vocalizing our emotions makes all the difference in the world," I poured out.

"Exactly," said Ayn. "The more people know about you, the better positioned they are to help you achieve what is important to you. The more you know about others, the better positioned you are to help them achieve what is important to them."

Then a light went on.

"The more I know about someone else, the more I will find in common with that person," I said. If we have the same fears, concerns, needs, desires, and even other emotions, we will probably relate better to each other. The better we understand each other, the better we get along, and we are in a position to build stronger relationships.

"Yes," Ayn replied softly, "You are completely right. Now think beyond your friends and family, your neighborhood, your school where you work, and even your community. What happens if not only people but countries also communicated this way."

"World peace?" I snickered a little bit thinking of the typical beauty pageant answer.

"Don't snicker," Ayn piped in. "That's exactly it."

The look in Ayn's eyes told me that he was completely serious. I could feel his demeanor, and I became quiet. The magnitude of just this first concept, this first commandment, was awesome. What if the world could achieve peace? What if our resources could be spent on food, shelter, and health facilities instead of weapons either to attack others or defend ourselves? *What would our world be like,* I wondered.

Ayn unrolled the scroll farther and continued to read.

Yesod... Foundation.

Thou shalt live a life
filled with balance and
grounded stability.

CHAPTER 13

*"**Yesod**... Foundation.*
Thou shalt live a life filled with
balance and grounded stability."

"The world has become an all-or-nothing place. People are so caught up with issues in their lives that they have forgotten that they need to feed their mind, body, and soul," Ayn explained.

I thought a moment before speaking this time.

"I live in a country where the people overeat, but they underread. We continuously feed our bellies and fail to continue feeding our minds. It's as if once we are out of school we don't need to read anymore because we know everything. The vast majority of people don't read a nonfiction book after their last day of formal education," I stated.

Ayn said, "Yes, that's right, but they also don't take care of their bodies or their spiritual selves.

And it goes much deeper than these areas. There are people who exercise seven days a week, but they don't spend the appropriate amount of time with their families. There are people who run seventy miles a week training for a marathon, but they never take the time to read books with their children or take a walk with their spouse."

"And, there are people who take better care of their car than the people in their communities who really need help," I added.

"That's just it," Ayn stated. "We have to stop living in a vacuum. We have to realize that life is meant to be a balance of needs with a balance of activities designed to satisfy those needs. But there's more. We have to learn to combine patience with balance. People not only want to focus on a very few needs in their life rather than live a balanced life, but they also want to achieve everything at once. Now!"

Another light went on in my head. "When we focus on trying to achieve it all so quickly, then we tend to ignore everything else in our lives," I added. "We want something so badly and want it right now, so we sacrifice everything and everyone else. It's the ultimate in selfishness."

"And what is the opposite of selfishness?" Ayn asked.

"Self*less*ness," I responded.

"Balance also means looking not only at your needs and desires but the needs and desires of the people around you—your family, your loved ones, and the community in which you live. People who only strive to balance their lives and not seek to be in balance with others are not living selfless lives."

"So not only do I need to work to balance my needs, but also to balance my needs with respect to the needs of others and the world we live in," I stated.

Ayn summed it up, "By being more patient and balancing all the areas of life and the activities within those areas, people will be healthier, happier, and richer. And, by balancing our needs with the needs of others, we will continue to serve while we also strive to be our best. If you don't have a stable foundation, you increase the likelihood of missing out on significant and valuable experiences. Living a balanced life provides us with a stable foundation. Without a balanced and stable foundation, you cannot achieve your full potential."

Tiferet... Beauty.

Thou shalt recognize that
there is true beauty in
the world and that you
are part of that beauty.

CHAPTER 14

*"**Tiferet**... Beauty.*
Thou shalt recognize that there is
true beauty in the world and that
you are part of that beauty."

"I haven't looked in the mirror lately, but I don't imagine that I am so 'beautiful' right now," I quipped.

"Well, I guess it matters in which light you are seen that determines how you really look. Similar to how a home movie shot in poor light will look bad, the people and the world in which we live appear the same way. If on the other hand we look at things in a good light, then everything looks great."

"It's all based on our point of reference," I added, but I didn't really understand where we were going.

Ayn continued, "Many times we simply see what we want to see. If we want to see the good in people, we see that; but if we only seek the negative attributes that people have, then that is all we ever see. If we see the beauty in people, then we will look at them differently, communicate with them differently, and treat them differently. People fall in love every day with other beautiful people. They fall in love because these people are able to see the real beauty that resides in their mates. Why were they able to see the tremendous beauty in that person while others were not?"

"Different reference points?" I answered.

"Yes, that's exactly right. We all look at people and life with a different reference point. We have different experiences and different definitions for what beauty is. But we must look beyond our personal definitions and realize that beauty is inherent in all people. We must not try and decide if someone is or isn't beautiful, but rather try and recognize where the beauty comes from in each person we meet. Everyone must stop judging others and recognize that all people have their own strengths and sources of beauty."

"What about the beauty in the world around us? What about the mountains, streams and forests?" I asked.

"Excellent point. Beauty does not just reside in people. It resides in everything around us. There is beauty in all of nature, not just in the mountains, but also in the animals that live on those mountains. We can simply enjoy the experience of walking through the fields, swimming in the lakes, and hiking in the forests, but ultimately we must realize that we are the guardians for all that beauty. The people of the world must all take responsibility for protecting that beauty. You don't just protect it for your enjoyment, you also protect it for long-term survival. Just as you must achieve balance in your personal life, balance in nature must also exist. If you bleed the earth of all of its beauty and resources, how will future generations of people survive?"

I said, "I realize how easy it is to just take and not give back. We cut a tree for firewood, but do we plant a new tree for someone else's firewood in the future? It really is an issue of personal responsibility. We each have an obligation to support and maintain the natural beauty that exists in our world and then to turn over this planet to the next generation in an equal or better condition than the way we received it. There is an additional challenge though."

"What is that?" Ayn asked.

"Cost. There is a cost associated with maintaining the condition of our planet. Many people are not willing to sacrifice for the sake of our planet."

"What is the cost of neglecting the earth in which you live? It can be hard to see the long-term benefits and justify the short-term sacrifice; but if you do not look long term, time will run out for everyone," said Ayn.

Netzach... Victory.
Thou shalt work with
passion and energy to
achieve significance.

CHAPTER 15

*"**Netzach**... Victory.*
Thou shalt work with passion and
energy to achieve significance."

"You are a university professor, no?"

I nodded yes.

"Do you love what you do? Do you put a piece of yourself into every lesson you prepare? Do you labor for hours to find meaningful material, create new approaches, plan intriguing assignments? Or, do you just slap something together on your way into class? It gets the job done and the dean doesn't sit in on your lectures anyway. So why bother?"

"I love to teach. Of course I prepare substantial lessons. At least I attempt to. I hope my students would agree," I said.

"Devote yourself to what you do. Don't spread yourself too thin between commitments; when you do, you cannot have the energy you need to be successful in each area of your life. And when you do commit, go all in. A commitment is not a maybe. A commitment is absolute. Find things in your personal and professional life about which you are passionate. Dedicate yourself to them, and you will see a difference in how you feel about your endeavors," Ayn admonished.

We sat in silence for a moment as I took in what Ayn said and he attempted to catch his breath. He was looking rather tired.

Ayn continued before I had a chance to speak, "Go the extra step, the extra mile. Do not do simply because you have to, but because you want to," he said. "Go above and beyond in order to excel and to make a difference through your actions. You have the ability to affect others and to improve the lives of those around you because of not only what you say and do, but also how you say and do them.

"And, success is not enough. You must work to achieve significance. Significance is the true victory. Significance has a far greater impact on the people around you. Furthermore, it is not enough to merely take the necessary steps to get the job done. It is critical that we are dedicated to not only the end product, but also to the journey we pursue on our way toward achieving the end goal."

"But as long as we end up at the same place..." I began before being cut off.

"It is not about the end," he repeated patiently. "You are always in a hurry, rushing to get to the next place, to do the next chore. Take some time to look around you and enjoy the scenery. It is all about the process. Too often this process, this journey, is disregarded as no one has time for it. Take a deep breath. Look around you. Forget, for just a minute, about the fifteen things that are constantly glaring at you from the top of your To-Do List. Enjoy where you are in life."

"Stop rushing. There's no reason to be in such a hurry, where you are right now isn't so bad. A wise woman once said, 'You may run, stumble, drive or fly, but never lose sight of the reason for the journey, or miss a chance to see a rainbow on the way.' The things we do in life are so rarely about the destination, but so rarely do we focus on the journey. By focusing on the journey, we may even enrich the destination and be able to enjoy it that much more. It was wisdom that was bestowed upon us all when it was said, 'It is good to have an end to journey toward, but it is the journey that matters in the end.'"

"Many people don't work hard to succeed, to enjoy victory in their endeavors," I said. "But, it also seems as if many people don't grow up believing that they can win. They are impoverished spiritually and financially, and they feel that this is the way life will always be. It is easier to be successful when it is modeled for you, when you are told it is possible, and when you see and believe it."

"Yes," Ayn said, "people must first know they can and will be successful. Then, they can work to move to the next and far more meaningful stage of being significant. Being significant means that you are not only impacting your life with your efforts, but also that you are impacting the lives of others in a very positive way.

"It is not just about accumulating resources. It is about how we use those resources to improve the world around us. Significance is about meaning and purpose. Ultimately achieving victory is accomplished through being significant. The impact you are having is incredible! Sam, you are not just

learning these words and ideas, you are truly understanding. I have chosen well."

Chesed...Loving-kindness.
Thou shalt treat all of
God's creatures with loving-
kindness so that the world
may function in harmony.

CHAPTER 16

*"**Chesed**...Loving-kindness.*
Thou shalt treat all of God's creatures
with loving-kindness so that the
world may function in harmony."

"Be nice to animals. Don't pollute or litter. Save the rainforest. Let's make peace for all of humankind. It sounds a little bit like what we teach our children in elementary school. Protect the environment, and be nice to everyone around you. We all know that it is important to protect the earth, or one day our children will not have an earth to protect. We've already mastered this commandment without even knowing it," I said confidently.

I probably should have known that Ayn would have something more substantial to add.

"What about the 'being nice to everyone around us' part? Have we mastered this concept?"

I took a moment to think before I responded. "In some ways, yes, but we have a lot left to do. There is fighting between countries from time to time, but it's about politics, and there is no way to stop people from having different opinions."

"What do you know about 'isms'?" Ayn inquired.

"Communism, socialism, Darwinism?"

"No, I mean more like ageism, racism, and sexism," said Ayn.

"You know, I hadn't really thought about all the forms of discrimination that people are forced to deal with on a regular basis. They are not ideals I learned as a child or taught my children as a parent. I know it exists in St. Louis, but I don't really experience it on a regular basis. I'm very lucky."

Ayn nodded his head and continued, "So clearly, we have not yet mastered the idea of treating everyone fairly, taking care of everyone and everything around us. There are so many acts of hatred that occur on a regular basis around the world, like child slavery in undeveloped nations, fighting over land, killing of innocent people.

"The more I think of it, there are plenty of problems in our own backyards as well. Not all children learn to love instead of hate. I hope that mine have, but there are so many people who breed hatred, instilling it within their children from day one. We cannot possibly achieve the harmony you spoke of until we learn to love and respect all of God's creatures. We must act with *kavod,* respect, treating others with the utmost respect and receiving it in return. Hatred is not an innate quality that some people are born with. Hatred and intolerance are taught. It is our responsibility to help prevent them from being passed from one generation to the next."

"But how?" I asked.

"Stop spreading hatred by starting to teach loving-kindness and don't tolerate hatred in others. If someone speaks from a position of hate or of ignorance, you will have to stand up and let them know that you will not accept that way of thinking. When you allow someone to say something that disrespects people, even when they act as if they are saying it in jest, and you say nothing, you might as well be endorsing the person's statement. If enough people speak out, then change will happen. You must speak out!"

Chochma...Wisdom.

Thou shalt strive to elevate your thinking to a level characterized by intuitive insight, deeper perception, knowledge and good judgement.

CHAPTER 17

"**Chochma**...Wisdom.
Thou shalt strive to elevate your
thinking to a level characterized by
intuitive insight, deeper perception,
knowledge and good judgement."

Ayn was going really long with this one.

"Be smart. I understand," I said.

"No, you don't. It's not about being smart. Anyone can be smart. Read a book. Watch the news. Go to school. Memorize spelling words, facts, or places on a map, and you are smart. Be able to take information, your own personal experiences, and the experiences of others, both living and dead, and then make better choices, share insights to help others, and avoid problems. *That* is wisdom. Wisdom is information and knowledge combined with time. When you gain wisdom, you look below the surface for deeper meaning and ways to apply the knowledge you have," he admonished.

I paused and thought about my grandfather, Opa. I had always looked up to him. Sure I thought he was smart, but what always seemed to catch my attention were the insights he shared. It was his wisdom that was so attractive. It was his wisdom that enabled him to smuggle his family out of Nazi-controlled Germany. It was his wisdom that allowed him to come to a new country, unable to speak the language, and build a good life for his family.

"You can't just choose to be wise," I boldly told Ayn.

Ayn smiled. "You're right. It takes time and effort. You need patience, and you also need to learn to see things differently. The first step is to recognize that there is a difference between being smart and being wise. The next step is to live your life seeking wisdom. First seek wisdom in others, and then seek wisdom in yourself. Once you begin to notice wisdom in other people, you will begin learning from their wisdom. The wisdom of others will permeate you first. Then you start to deepen your thought process and build a foundation of wisdom within yourself.

"You must be aware of how information and experiences relate to one another and possess the ability to affect future decisions. It may not be there at first, but one day you will wake up, face an issue, or be presented with an opportunity to give someone advice, and you will sense that you used wisdom in that instance."

"Then I'll be wise?" I asked.

"No. Then you have used wisdom. Gaining wisdom is a never-ending life journey. It's not a matter of wise or not. You may gain and use wisdom, but that is just the beginning of the process. Your wisdom grows over time. Never stop seeking wisdom."

Hod...Commitment.

Thou shalt be accountable for
your values and live every
day with determination
and perseverance.

CHAPTER 18

*"**Hod**...Commitment.*
Thou shalt be accountable for your
values and live every day with
determination and perseverance."

"If you were pushed over the side of a very tall building and you were able to grab a railing before falling fifty stories to the street and certain death, how hard would you hold on until help came?"

I replied, "I would hold on with all my might. My hands would have to almost fall off before I would give in and let go. If there was any chance to survive, I would do anything in my power to do so."

"That's commitment," Ayn said. "You would be committed to living and you would hold on as long as humanly possible. We have talked about sovereignty, foundation, beauty, victory, loving-kindness and wisdom. Now is where commitment comes in.

You must be willing to do everything in your power, known and unknown, to achieve and live by these commandments. Talking about them, writing them down, and expressing your feelings about them is fine. However, it is *hod,* this extreme commitment and accountability to yourself and your values that determines your success.

"But, it goes beyond that. You must commit yourself to everything you do. Don't do something unless you are going to give it everything you have. You don't want to be known for just getting the job done. You want to be known for giving your best every time!

"A commitment is *no matter what.* When you make a commitment to yourself or to anyone else, it means that you will keep your commitment—no matter what. A commitment is not a maybe. It is definite. It is absolute. It is no matter what!"

"I always try to be as perfect as possible," I added hoping to satisfy Ayn.

"That is not what I'm talking about. Perfection impedes action. If you want to be perfect or do the perfect job, you will always wait for the 'perfect' moment to begin. Since there is no perfect moment to begin any endeavor, you may not start, and you won't accomplish anything at all. Don't strive for perfection. Strive for excellence. Do a great job and don't worry if it is perfect. If you do excellent work, if it is to the absolute best of your ability, it will always be acceptable, and you will always be happy with your results," Ayn stated.

"So," I said, "I need to commit to every project using all of my skills, develop new skills if necessary, and don't worry about being perfect. Focus on staying with the project or life concept with my full commitment, and always be accountable to my values. And, do my absolute best—no matter what! Right?"

"Yes, that's correct. It is simple in concept but difficult to consistently implement. But, you can do it. And, there are other commitments. It is not just the commitments you make to yourself and your pursuits. The commitments you make to the people in your life are critical. You become known for keeping your commitments. You build trust with others by keeping your commitments. You show the people around you that you are dependable, that they can always count on you, because you always, no matter what, keep your commitments to them.

Hod is the glue that will bring all of the commandments to life for you. It is what will make everything real in your life. A no-matter-what commitment is very powerful. Commitment and accountability will help you through the tough times that all people who achieve significance eventually face. It means that nothing matters more than *why* you are striving to achieve your goals and that no amount of time will keep you from achieving the significance you desire."

Ayn paused to catch his breath. I wish I had some water to offer him. It had been a long day, and I was amazed that at his age he could accomplish everything that he did. It was a tough climb, and he was putting his entire being into teaching me what he had to share. After the brief pause, he continued.

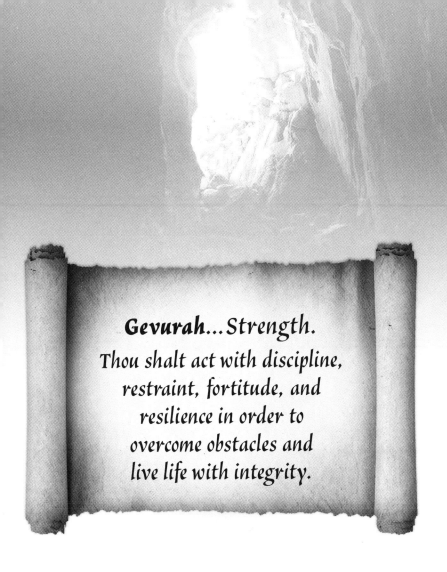

Gevurah...Strength.

Thou shalt act with discipline,
restraint, fortitude, and
resilience in order to
overcome obstacles and
live life with integrity.

CHAPTER 19

*"**Gevurah**... Strength.*
Thou shalt act with discipline,
restraint fortitude and resilience
in order to overcome obstacles
and live life with integrity."

"So, do you ever lift weights?" Ayn asked. "Do you work out?"

"I run whenever possible," I responded. "Maybe three or four times a week. Twice a week my wife and I lift weights together."

"What is the result of those workout?"

"Well, it's supposed to be good for my health. I feel good. And when I participate in other activities like skiing or hiking, I find that I'm stronger and able to do more than some of my friends. Strengthening my body helps me participate in physical activities at a higher level."

"That makes sense," Ayn acknowledged. "Strengthening your body helps you complete physical activities at a higher level. But strengthening your *mind* allows you to complete *all* tasks and activities at a higher level."

"Where does mental strength come from? It's not like you can take your mind to the gym to get a workout," I quipped.

"Mental strength comes from combining hod, or the commitment and self-accountability we talked about, with discipline. Discipline means doing what you know is right even when it is the hard choice to make. Discipline means doing what is right even when you want to do something else. Commitment and discipline create strength. This strength is what helps you deal with tough times and gets you to the good times."

"But how do you *work out* to develop this strength?" I asked.

"Well, you can't go to the gym. That's for sure."

"Then where do I go?"

"You go out into the real world. You face real situations and make real choices. You use mental discipline, along with choices that come from your heart, because in your heart you usually know what is right and what is wrong. When your choices are based on your values, they are inherently better choices."

"So that's it?" I asked.

"No, there's more," Ayn stated. "The goal is to live with integrity. Integrity is a higher level of choices and actions. It comes from aligning your words with your actions. It is not enough to say you believe in something. Your actions must show that you are committed to your ideals."

"Making the tough decisions that I know are right even when everyone around me is choosing to do what they really want, but might not be right, is going to build strength?" I asked.

"Yes, mental strength. You are strengthening your mind and building integrity. And, you are building your reputation at the same time. You are building a reputation that says, 'I am someone who does the right thing even though it is the tough decision. I can be counted on when times are tough. I will be there when someone needs me. When I say I will do something that always means, no matter what. When everyone and everything around me is enveloped in chaos, I will be steady, dependable, and consistently reliable.'"

Ayn continued, "Ultimately, people want to associate with people who live with integrity. People want to do business with people who live with integrity and with companies whose guiding principles are based in integrity. Integrity may seem like the tough choice on the surface and the slow road to success, but integrity is really the only proven road to significance. When you live your life with integrity, you develop strength. Strength that will serve you well always."

Binah...Understanding.

Thou shalt listen to others' thoughts and feelings and work to fully comprehend other people's ideas and beliefs.

CHAPTER 20

*"**Binah**...Understanding.
Thou shalt listen to others'
thoughts and feelings and
work to fully comprehend other
people's ideas and beliefs."*

"Sam, have you ever talked with people who wanted to own the conversation? They had to be the ones talking, and when you did say something, they usually cut you off."

"Sure. It's no fun. I'd rather talk with someone else," I said.

"Right. They take the fun out of the conversation. They are rude. And ultimately, they are not listening to you. They are more concerned with their situation, their challenges, and their issues in life.

"If you don't work to understand what is going on with the people around you, then you can't possibly do anything to help them. You won't be capable of providing them with something that will be appreciated in their life. In other words, you will be unable to be significant to the people around you."

"I can't take care of everyone around me. It's enough to help take care of my four children," I blurted out. The moment those words left my mouth I knew I was in for a piece of Ayn's mind.

"I guess no one ever looked out for you, gave you a helping hand, provided for you or made sure you were in a safe secure place?" Ayn asked. "You have accomplished everything in your life on your own, by yourself, and without the help of anyone else?"

Well, I knew the true answers to all of those questions. *I've had plenty of help over the years from my parents, friends, and ultimately my wife,* I thought.

Ayn continued on, "We must all work to listen to others. It is not enough to just hear them. We must learn to understand the other peoples of the world, those who are in our local communities and around the world. As we better understand them, we can better help them achieve what they feel they need to achieve. By understanding better, we can serve better. And when we serve others and help them improve their lives, we are improving the world. And then what happens, Sam?" Ayn asked.

"I guess if the world in which we live is better as a whole, then it's better for each of us as individuals too," I answered.

"Right. By serving others, you are simultaneously improving your own position, without even trying. What could be more noble than that?" Ayn said.

"But it's not enough to just want to help others. We have to learn about them first. We need to understand people before we can lend a hand. And the only way that happens is to ask questions and to listen to their thoughts, opinions, and feelings without worrying about being the one speaking. And when you listen, don't judge, just listen. This is key in order to understand people. It is also critical to building good relationships. We cannot help individuals to improve their lives or to improve our communities unless we truly understand one another," he said.

"Listening without judging is a hard thing to do sometimes," I commented. "We want so badly to express ourselves. We want to be right. We want to look smart. Most people feel that when they are speaking they are in control of the conversation, and that that's a good thing. Oddly enough, that is exactly the opposite of the truth. We learn when we listen, not when we speak."

"And you have been listening and learning so well," Ayn responded. "It's time to cover the last remaining commandment."

Keter...Crown.
Thou shalt recognize that
all people have within them
a spark of the divine.

CHAPTER 21

*"**Keter**...Crown.*
Thou shalt recognize that
all people have within them
a spark of the divine."

"All human beings are created in the image of the divine. Do you know what this means?" asked Ayn.

"We all look like God?" I answered with a question.

"No," Ayn said flatly.

"God looks like us?" I asked.

"No," Ayn repeated. "It is not about looks. It is not about our physical being. We don't have God's looks," he almost scoffed. "We all have God's essence. We are each created with a bit of God inside of us."

"What an empowering concept," I thought aloud.

Then Ayn asked, "If I told you that you had the opportunity to meet God, how would you react?"

"Wow," I blurted out. "That would be incredible!"

"Why?" Ayn asked.

"Because I have so many questions. There is so much I want to learn, and there is only one being that could teach that to me. What an opportunity!" I exclaimed.

Then Ayn presented a scenario. "If you were taken to a mountain top, brought inside a magnificent palace, placed in front of a set of very large doors, and told that behind the set of doors God awaited you, what would you feel?"

"My heart would be racing, that's for sure," I replied.

"When you entered the room with God, what emotions would you possess?" Ayn asked.

"Respect, honor, humility, amazement," the words continued to flow from my tongue, "admiration, awe, elation."

Ayn then asked, "If you feel that way about being in God's presence, and if every human being has the essence of God in them, how should you feel about, and treat, all the people of this earth?"

A new silence engulfed me. I was starting to see exactly where Ayn was going. I felt so dumb. Racing to my mind were all the times I prejudged someone or drew conclusions that were not based on facts or thought ill about people because they looked or acted different.

"Why go to the effort of thinking negatively about people when we can admire them for their differences and learn from them?" I asked rhetorically. "If we go into every relationship with the same feelings I just described, I bet we would build positive relationships instead of dismissing people for no reason at all. If people look different from me, I must look different to them, and I wouldn't want them to prejudge me."

"But this is much bigger than you and the way you personally treat people," Ayn said. "How many millions of people have been killed throughout time because of where they lived, how they looked, or what they believed? Why are men and women so worried about what others believe in, wear, or worship? People kill in the name of religion, sovereignty, and the betterment of man. It is ridiculous!

It is based on ego and insecurity rather than respect and caring. That kind of logic just does not hold water. You should treat all people—no matter their nationality, race, religion, or other belief structure—as the divine beings they were created as. Now show me one good reason to fight, kill, or go to war. If all the time, money, and other resources that were spent in destructive actions were focused on world health, food, and quality of life, what would happen to the people of this earth?"

I responded, "This is really big. What a powerful idea. I can see how this single concept could change the way not only I look at people, but also how everyone treats each other. If we are all created with a piece of the Divine inside us, and if we respect the Divine, then we must respect each other."

"Right!" injected Ayn. "But there is even more. Since the spark of the Divine is within you, you must also treat yourself with that same respect, honor your individual gifts, and above all else know that even though you are not a perfect being, you are a perfect you. You must always honor your authentic self. And if you have feelings of lack, you have just forgotten your connection to Divine abundance.

"And one more thing. Because the Divine has the ability to create, then you too have the ability to create. You create first in your mind and then in the real world. Anything that has ever been created was first created in someone's mind. You must see it first in your mind and then you make it a reality. This is true if you are creating a building, a machine, or even creating a world and community where people support each other and where the goal is being the best you can be.

"If you take nothing else away, if you are only able to teach one concept to the people you come in contact with, this single idea could change the world. It would eliminate so much pain and suffering and produce so much joy and peace. You must recommit to taking this message and giving it to everyone you can," Ayn concluded.

CHAPTER 22

I had totally lost track of time. There was no way we would be getting back to the car today. We had been in the cave for hours, but, amazingly, I wasn't that tired.

"Let's sleep here tonight and return in the morning," Ayn said. "I found these blankets in the corner."

As I crawled under my blanket, I listened to Ayn's words.

"You have studied and learned well," he said. "Now you must do something with your knowledge. These ten lost commandments can bring riches to anyone. Fulfill your promise, and share them with the world. All people need these commandments."

As I drifted off to sleep I reviewed *The Ten Lost Commandments* in my mind:

Malkhut... Sovereignty.
Thou shalt share thyself
with others by expressing
your authentic emotions
and thoughts.

Yesod... Foundation.
Thou shalt live a life
filled with balance and
grounded stability.

Tiferet... Beauty.
Thou shalt recognize that
there is true beauty in
the world and that you
are part of that beauty.

Netzach... Victory.
Thou shalt work with
passion and energy to
achieve significance.

Chesed...Loving-kindness.
Thou shalt treat all of
God's creatures with loving-
kindness so that the world
may function in harmony.

Chochma...Wisdom.
Thou shalt strive to
elevate your thinking to
a level characterized by
intuitive insight, deeper
perception, knowledge,
and good judgement.

Hod...Commitment.
Thou shalt be accountable to
your values and live every
day with determination
and perseverance.

Gevurah... Strength.
Thou shalt act with
discipline, restraint,
fortitude, and resilience in
order to overcome obstacles
and live life with integrity.

Binah... Understanding.
Thou shalt listen to
others' thoughts and
feelings and work to fully
comprehend other people's
ideas and beliefs.

Keter... Crown.
Thou shalt recognize that
all people have within them
a spark of the Divine.

I realized that these commandments, the second ten, were not about what *not to do,* but about
what we should be doing, how we should live our

lives, and how we should treat all people. I felt empowered by my newfound appreciation and understanding of the first ten commandments and by my knowledge of the second ten. They gave me guidance, provided a foundation on which I could build my life, and emerged as a potential source of strength. I felt better equipped to make good decisions throughout my life, because I had something concrete to draw from.

A sense of energy surged through my body as I realized what I had been given. Ayn had shared a tremendous gift with me, and he was right. By living life based on all twenty principles, anyone could earn riches. They could earn riches in their emotional life, their spiritual life, and certainly in their physical life. The key was not just to know these ten additional commandments, but to also implement them into our lives, to live them day in and day out, and to make better choices based on them. The last thing I remembered Ayn saying was, "Share these—you will do well."

And I fell asleep.

CHAPTER 23

I felt Ayn's warm touch on my face. I drifted somewhere between the sound sleep I desired and wakefulness I dreaded.

Please let me sleep just a little bit longer, I thought.

I was tired and wanted to sleep, but Ayn must have been waking me early for the trip home. I rolled over in an effort to avoid the inevitable. Then I rolled back over. The warmth would not leave, and my blanket felt unusually soft. No one was touching my face, yet the warmth was still there. It felt just like the sun through the skylights in my bedroom at home. I opened my eyes and bolted upright in my bed. "My bed?! How could this be?" I said aloud. *I just fell asleep in the cave. How could I be in my bed, in my house?* I thought, perplexed.

I jumped out of bed, grabbed my watch, and ran into the kitchen. No one was home.

"Where's the calendar," I shouted, as I tore through Renee's kitchen desk.

At last I found it and opened it up to the day indicated by the number on my watch. It was Tuesday, the Tuesday before spring break. I couldn't believe it. What about the trip to Israel? What about my speech? More importantly, what about Ayn and the lost commandments? Was it just an endless dream, with no apparent beginning or satisfying conclusion?

I was distraught.

"It seemed so real," I said to myself as I slipped on my running shorts and shoes.

I had gone to Israel, met Ayn, given my speech, traveled into the desert, and studied the ten lost commandments with Ayn. There were too many details for this to be just a dream. My head spun as if it were on a stick. I didn't know what to think anymore, so I went out the door for my morning run. Maybe that would help clear my head.

It didn't. I returned home with just as many unanswered questions as when I had left. As I walked through the house, I stopped at the fireplace mantle. There was Renee's collection of porcelain clowns. No shofar in sight.

I dressed, picked up my briefcase by the door, and got into my car. I left the radio off for the drive to campus. I couldn't believe that everything I had experienced was just a dream. Ayn was so real, so kind, so important to me. It was all so vivid. Now it was all gone. I felt as if I had been robbed of a prized possession. I felt grief over losing a friend. I was frustrated. I was angry.

After parking my car, I walked to my building, went by my office, checked my mail, and hung up my coat. Then, I headed down the hall to my class-room. Students filled all the chairs, and I opened my briefcase to retrieve my lesson plan. As I opened the case, a familiar aroma filled my nose. It was a sort of stale, musty smell. The familiarity of this smell made the small hairs on the back of my neck stand on end. I looked down. There inside my brief-case was a pile of papers—old pieces of parchment with my handwriting on them.

I picked up the first sheet and then the second. I rifled through the stack of papers like a kid trying to eat his cookie as fast as possible so he could get more before the bag was empty. Here, in my brief-case, were all the notes I took in the cave. I held in my hands all of the lost commandments, and all of the thoughts that Ayn and I shared about them.

The last sheet of paper had one simple sentence on it. It was not in my handwriting. It simply said, *"Share these—you will do well."* It was signed, *Ayn.* It couldn't have all been a dream. Ayn did exist. He was real.

But who is he? I asked myself.

Regardless of my confusion, I knew then that I was charged with the responsibility of sharing the lost commandments with the entire world.

And so I began.

ACKNOWLEDGMENTS

I would like to thank my daughter Sara Ferrara for the phenomenal editing and insights she provided. I would also like to thank David Wildasin. You knew the importance of this project and you backed it all the way. I am forever grateful.

Bring Sam Silverstein to Your Organization

Contact Us

Sam Silverstein, Incorporated

121 Bellington Lane

St. Louis, Missouri 63141

info@SamSilverstein.com

(314) 878-9252

Fax: (314) 878-1970

To Order More Copies of *The Lost Commandments:*

www.samsilverstein.com

Follow Sam

www.twitter.com/samsilverstein

www.youtube.com/samsilverstein

www.linkedin.com/in/samsilverstein